ANNEXATION

UNFAZED PUBLISHING
YOUR MIND IS OUR BUSINESS

TAMPA FLORIDA

QUENTIN A. BOSTON

ISBN: 978-1-959275-27-5

Library of Congress Number: 2023938964

UNFAZED PUBLISHING
YOUR MIND IS OUR BUSINESS

TABLE OF CONTENTS

TABLE OF CONTENTS

ANNEXATION

----------- Chapter 1-----------

"Dream Tale"

Hi, my name is 5. This world I live in isn't a dream world or fairytale. I live on the planet Xeno. Formally known as planet earth before the invasion. Earth was invaded about one hundred fifty years ago and most of the human population has been destroyed. After the rebellion settled, we escaped the camps. Fighting for our lives we've been surviving. Making the aliens respect us. When we were invaded one hundred fifty years ago, three races of aliens went to war over our planet. The three races are the Trolls, Invitca, and The Risen. The Trolls are the most physically blessed. Their skin is like steel. They have very huge hands and on average are ten feet tall. They were second to invade and didn't hate humans right away. We had an alliance, but a bomb exploded destroying their capital during a civil union. Our alliance was over. They vowed to destroy everything about us and erase the human race from existence.

The Invitca have been here for centuries. They implemented themselves by getting into very high positions in every government. By disguising themselves they rose to power. They made the most powerful governments go bankrupt and collapse. Making us rely on them, they made us serve them as slaves. They hate the Trolls. The Invitca are not that much taller than the average human being about five foot five. They are extremely fast though, and can change parts of their bodies in to anything they need. Making them extremely dangerous. They didn't really need weapons because they are weapons.

The Risen were last to invade. By the time they arrived, the last of the humans had already escaped the camps. The Invitca made humans into "Dream Walkers." Dream Walkers are mindless soldiers who had special abilities. We called them zombies.

They used these mindless zombies to help fight against the Trolls. The Risen loved this idea and wanted to make their own human soldiers to go to war with the Invitca. The Risen are dark red and can fly. They are on average about seven feet tall. However, their strength rivals the Trolls. They hate every race on Xeno and their goal is to destroy everyone. They want the planet and will do anything to be the only race remaining.

The year is 2450 and I am one of the human high ranking officials. I fight for freedom, but also peace. My mom is Half Invitca and Risen, and my dad is half Troll and human. This makes me one of the few people out here mixed with everything, but I look completely human. I just want to bring peace to Xeno so that my kids will not have to fight in this war one day.

My friends and I were just about to board the train when BOOM! The train station went up in smoke and fire. A bright mushroom filled the sky above as the sunny day was filled with dirt and ash. My body flew into the air flipping my head colliding into a wall. Before passing out, all I could hear were the cries of my people. This station was supposed to be an entente cordiale. Moments later I woke up from another explosion realizing what happened. My body was aching. I could feel the warmth of my blood dripping down from my head. Panic over took me. Where is my team? I was barely able to raise up on my feet. Swaying from side to side, I finally caught my balance. Everything around me was engulfed in flames. Embers were burning my skin as I got on my feet. Moving now as best as I could, I couldn't breathe. The air was almost suffocating. It feels as if my heart was beating out of my chest. Feeling every pulse getting heavier and heavier. The wind racing across my face. I ran past the Trolls that were gorging on the dead humans. I cloaked myself in enlightenment making sure to avoid them. I caught a glimpse of my partners and stopped running.

"Martin, where is Shoya?"

He looks ahead and pointed in the distance. I turned my head to focus. She was about four miles away at the end of a train station. My heart sunk to the bottom of my stomach. I saw Shoya fighting a Troll general that has been enlightened. Enlightenment is a source of power that comes from Xeno. It can be used in many ways. This Troll was ten foot four and very muscular. He had enlightenment running through his veins using it to amplify his strength and speed. Shoya is a hybrid; half machine and half Invitca. She's five foot seven with crystal blue skin. The machinery changed the color of her skin.

I ran full speed using my enlightenment getting me to about 140 mph. He grabbed and slammed her with full might. Her body bounced off the ground as the air escaped her lungs. She gained side to side. You could see a cloud of dust rise. He grabbed her throat trying to crush it. Shoya starts to fear as she began losing air to her brain. She starts to feel her heart beat getting stronger. She suddenly gets an idea. Shoya hits him with a heart vibration through her hands. This shakes the inside of his body at a high velocity. He loosened his grip dropping her. The vibration wasn't strong enough to do any real damage since Trolls have thicker skin. They take less damage than most making it harder to face them in battle. He grabs her hands crushing her wrists. I heard her bones cracking from a distance. She screamed out this horrible cry. It broke my soul as I listened.

"I'm almost there. Just hold on."

I tried to yell out, but dread stopped the words from leaving my mouth. I released all of my energy into the bottom of my feet. I jumped sending myself flying through the air. I gathered my enlightenment into my fist. BLAM!!! I connected! Slamming his head into the ground. The blood already running from his eye splattered. The ground cracked from the impact. Trains that were destroyed were blown backwards. Shoya jumped and blasted him with a heart disruption. It wasn't as strong because her wrists were broken. I could see the pain from using that move again. The portal the Troll used was starting to close. Shoya picked him up letting out a huge cry from the pain, and threw him back in. Since he was a general, sending him back took all the other Trolls. They're all linked together by their blood for some reason. Making it easier for them to travel in groups.

"Are you okay Shoya?" 5 asked.

Shoya had been badly injured. She had a broken arm and a couple of cracked ribs with her broken wrists. It will take her longer to heal since she is a hybrid and may need new parts.

----------- Chapter 2 -----------

"Lost Times"

I enjoy waking up hearing the birds chirping. The nature that surrounds me was up and alive. The wind howled through the leaves of the trees nearby. While looking at my children sleeping in peace, my mind drifted to when I was a child. My mother and I would spend a lot of time together. She would teach me the important things in life. One thing she would often tell me was, "Even though we are different, we all are the same. One earth one mind."

She would teach me many things while we cleaned up our house. Mother would share old tapes of the world before the invasion. Before everything got turned upside down. She showed me, "The Lost Tapes Of Hope." That's what she called them. I was seeing people going to the beach, to amusement parks, and everyone was joyful. Everything was so peaceful.

I started thinking about life today, and how everything had changed. My oldest is my daughter Zaya who is fourteen, and takes more after me than her mother. My son, her younger brother, Ryan was only twelve and still hasn't developed his enlightenment. They make me so proud to be a father. I remember when my wife was pregnant. She kept saying that I would be a great father. I hoped to be as great as my dad. I must protect them. I remember holding them for the first time. Zaya held my finger so tightly, and Ryan, on the other hand, was full of laughter. I worry for my children. We are the abominations that the pure humans hate. I'm looked down upon by most of them because I am a mixture of every race; and so are my children. So at night I stay up and watch over them making sure we didn't get attacked. I really enjoy watching the birds during sun rise. I spend my time thinking about how life has triggered various horrible memories.

It made me remember how my parents died. We

were attacked by the human leader at that time. The human leader and my father fought intensely. Apparently, the human leader and my dad both wanted my mom. My mom chose my dad which pissed the leader off. Once I came along they thought he had gotten over it. They were wrong. Unfortunately, it was about to cost them both. One day everything felt off from the time I woke up to the time I closed my eyes. My mother suddenly woke me up, grabbed me by my wrist, and ran us into the forest. I was in a daze and very discombobulated as I witnessed tears in her eyes. I turned around and could see our house burning. Smoked covered everything. I could hear my father's battle cries and see his silhouette fighting.

"What is going on?" I thought to myself.

My father fought his hardest. Being half Troll gave him the advantage, but they outnumbered him and slowly destroyed him. I could hear the impacts of the brutal beating he was getting. I would look up at my mom and feel her tears landing on my head. She looked me in my eyes as she hid me in a cave. She told me, "Remember what I taught you. Your father and I will forever live on in your heart. I love you my son." My mother, madly in love, ran back at full speed. With her being half Invitca, she returned just in time to hold his hand before he took his last breath. His body had been torn to pieces and burnt. My dad tried to speak, but the smoke was choking him. My mom held him close with tears streaming down. His body was beaten so bad she couldn't move him without hurting him. She looked him in his eyes with deep compassion and love as her tears flowed,

"You were the best thing to ever happen to me. You gave me the best life you could. A great son. I love you with everything. I will not let you go alone my love."

My dad being exhausted exhaled for the last time. My mom proceeded to close his eyes. She paused for a moment as if she was focusing her thoughts. BOOM!!! An explosion erupted as my mom unlocked her enlightenment. Being filled with focused rage she was now functioning in pure hatred. She confronted the leader of the humans. Beating him to a pulp as he begged for his life. She laughed,

"I thought you had more dignity than this..., but you're just a coward. A dirty bitch."

She crushed his head. Tears continued from her eyes as her anger grew. The rest of the human leaders found her in the process of crushing his skull. They all had smirks on their faces. She didn't even want to explain herself. She started killing them all. Fighting to the death with all the human leaders. She killed most of them. My mom and the last human leader fought severely, and both took their last breath together. Well, at least this is what I was told while I was hidden in a cave.

I just wanted to know why she left me, but then

I remembered them saying to me, if one of them died, the other would die too. Being alive without my parents was just like dying. I was seven when this happened. I couldn't go back to the human territory. So I used the skills my father taught me. I fought for my life in the "Forest of Death." I lived there for years. When I was fourteen, I was chosen by the enlightenment. Enlightenment is something that almost everyone gets. It can be used in many different ways. It usually develops when you are in dire situations, however, it's rare that it chooses you. Humans don't know how enlightenment began; or is this a lie. Who's knows?

Earth being invaded brought a bunch of new wildlife that crossbreed with ours. Making strong hybrids and creating a bunch of new dangerous species. It was cool and bad at the same time. I fought every day of my life. This made me strong. It made me tough. I don't want to have to put my kids through this. They can be strong, but not from being left behind. I will not let this life my parents died for be for nothing. I had to come back to the humans because I wouldn't be accepted anywhere else. Yet, I do not trust them. I will not let my children have to see or feel what I've been through.

"Dad, what's for breakfast?" Ryan asked. I came back to reality before answering.

"I don't know. Whatever you want. Just go make it." I replied.

"Awe dad. Why do you make us make it? Awe dad, why don't you make us breakfast anymore?" Ryan asked again.

"Ryan, you are twelve now. You can make your own breakfast." I calmly suggested.

"Well, imma wake up Zaya to make me something to eat. Her food taste just like mom's." He started running over to her room. I walked in front of him.

"No, let her sleep. Y'all both have big days today, and honestly, you should be asleep."

----------- Chapter 3 -----------

"Trials"

Zaya finally woke up. Ryan had warmed him up some leftovers. She asked me.

"Dad, are you going to miss us while we're gone?"

Zaya was talking about the academy exam that she and Ryan had to participate in.

"Of course I'm going to miss you. Y'all have to stick together and watch each other's back. You must survive and come back to me." 5 stated.

Ryan chuckled in a worried tone. I could see the worry on his face.

"I know this is important, but Dad, we're your children. We'll be fine." Zaya said while grabbing something to eat.

Zaya and Ryan started getting ready after eating breakfast. I had a flash back to my first son.

confident, but he was stronger than me at that age. I am scared because I had a son named Zero. He took the exam ten years ago when he was twelve years of age. He would've been twenty two years of age, but he went missing. A lot of kids die in these exams. They are taken into the forest of death filled with dangerous animals, and now filled with our enemies of the other nations. This exam was to kind of force their enlightenment out. To develop them to be warriors so that we can defend the ill, old, and young. It is a rite of passage and it's mandatory. We found no remains of my son Zero, and no traces to follow. I hoped in my heart that he was still alive out there.

"Hey dad, are you okay?"

I snapped out of it. Zaya looked at me worried and Ryan seemed the same.

"I am okay. Just be safe my children."

I stood up and hugged them tightly. "They cannot be shielded anymore." I thought to myself. I did not tell them that they had an older brother. Zaya was a baby and didn't remember him. I, and their mother, made a pact not to tell them. It broke us, but we thought it was for the best. I love them with all of my heart and wished I could go with them. Zaya and Ryan left. I watched them leave with so much hope, but I worry in my heart.

"Zaya, we are going to ace this." Ryan said.

But looking back watching my dad, I could sense the worry from him.

"Ryan, you have to stay close by me in this exam. I will protect you." Zaya says confidently.

Ryan looked just as worried as our dad.

"I will protect you too Zaya. I promise." Ryan yelled with determination.

As we walked our classmates joined us. We were all laughing to hide our fear. We had many classmates who were upperclassmen who took the exam before us. They never returned. The trauma of those who did return scared us. To make this easier for us, they taught us to never learn each other's names. They said we can learn the names of those who return. We were trained based on the weapons that picked us. We went through a ceremony where there are weapons placed on the wall. We had to close our eyes, and the weapon would appear in front of us. Zaya opened her eyes to see her weapon was a staff. Ryan opened his eyes to see his weapon were these special brass knuckles. Our mom's weapon are flails and dad's dual swords.

Zaya had already unlocked her enlightenment through training. Dad would take us in the forest and make us fight for our dinner. Never letting us die of course, but never intervening unless he had to. Our weapons and enlightenment go hand in hand. Enlightenment isn't only used for our weapons, we can use it throughout our whole body.

The way our dad taught us to use our enlightenment was that it should flow naturally. Like water around boulders. Like the wind around a mountain. Let it be free inside of you and flow like nature.

Zaya was being so calm. I was terrified. Especially with dad acting as if we might die. They told us to fight like our lives are on the line. I didn't want my dad to cry or be devastated, and I didn't want to let my sister down. Our instructor came over and began talking to us.

"Hey everybody. Come here. These are the rules. You will be in pairs. You can pick your own partner. You will all ride on my Zoro. Jump off when we reach the point. When I point to you and your partner, that's your cue to jump off together. You must survive for two weeks. We will pick you up exactly where we dropped you off."

This was perfect. I looked at Ryan right away and we already knew we were a team. This gives me the best possible way to protect my brother. We boarded the Zoro. A Zoro is a giant bird that can only be seen by being above this bird. The bottom of this bird is camouflaged. We use these animals to be undetected by the aliens.

We took flight into the air and I felt the breeze run across my face. Ryan looked sick in the stomach, and fear set in the bottom of my stomach. They pointed to me. I looked Ryan dead in his eyes. I grabbed Ryan's hand and we jumped not knowing what's next as we descended upon our destiny.

----------- Chapter 4 -----------

"Changes"

"ZAYAAAAAA!!!!!!"

Ryan screamed at the top of his lungs. We were free falling together. The wind sounded as if it was screaming in my ears. I smiled as my heart filled with a sense of joy. A sense of freedom. Like a bird flying free from a cage for the first time. I let go of my brother so that I could dive faster. I filled my legs and arms with enlightenment to absorb the shock. The ground crumbled beneath my feet and I caught my brother. We were finally on the ground surrounded by wildlife. All we could hear were birds and bugs.

"Are you ready Ryan?"

"Yes Zaya!!! We can do it!!!"

(…Meanwhile back home.)

"Hey 5, what are you doing?"

Shoya had been in the shop after our fight with

the Troll. She needed new parts. Especially around her neck and rib area. I haven't seen her in two weeks. She was finally released and could walk around now on her own.

"How many days since the exam started at the academy?" Shoya asked.

"Shoya, it's been five days. To take the stress away I've been training. I've been pretty calm although what happened with Zero is on my mind. But to be honest, I would love to go out there and be with them."

"5, I understand that, but they have to spread their wings. You can't protect them forever. We are getting old now."

"Shoya, you are thirty seven, and I'm thirty eight. We are not old yet. I want to protect my kids until they have kids. Even still they will be my babies."

"5, I understand. How are you and your wife doing?"

"She is on a mission right now. I have been awaiting her return. You know she is a spy."

(...Back to Zaya and Ryan)

"ZAYA!!!"

"Please, please, don't be dead!! Please, Zaya don't be dead!!"

I was carrying her on my back running as fast as I could. I was being chased by The Risen. They were gaining on us. I took Zaya and hid her in a nearby cave. I had my brass knuckles applied around my hands.

"Hey boy! Come out! We can smell you. You disgusting mixed breed! Get out here you fucking mutt!"

I walked out of the cave. The only thing going through my mind was I had to protect Zaya. My heart was beating so fast. I felt my heartbeat throughout my entire body.

"What are you doing here you fucking mutt? You

better talk too. We've been killing your classmates. Not one of them said anything."

Ryan answered, "My school is participating in a survivor exam."

"Ohhhh. Soooo, …. you're trying to awaken your enlightenment, huh? I guess the three of us will have to kill you; son of 5! We will take your head and wear it!"

I wondered. How did they know my dad? How did they know I'm his son? And I haven't seen any of my classmates in days.

"How do you know who I am?" I asked being baffled at their knowledge.

One of them chuckled, "We killed everyone else in this forest. Y'all are the last two people alive from that class."

I became horrified! I liked this girl in my class who I played games with and spent time with at school.

I was going to ask her for her name when we returned. Then I heard a loud boom like thunder crackling. He appeared right beside me. Bang!! My face felt like fire as my head smacked the ground. I wasn't knocked out though.

"He's probably dead. Weak human mutt. Let's kill the girl next."

I jumped up punching the back of his head. It barely moved forward.

"Is that all you got mutt?"

He punched me in my stomach. I felt no pain. Only the air escaping my body as I was sent flying into a nearby tree. I felt hopeless. They all gathered together in laughter.

"Let's make a deal. If you can kill one of us, we will leave you alone. We promise. Unlike you lying humans. We keep our word."

I agreed because they were only scouts. I know for a fact I could win. They formed a triangle and started glowing. Becoming one they said,

"You have no hope of beating us now."

The Risen have a technique that allows them to combine and form. A bright light shined as they disappeared from my sight. Boom!!!!! They shattered my ribs in the blink of an eye. Their hand was as big as my legs combined. It was now wrapped around my chest. Not killing me, but holding me. "I think this is what dying feels like." I thought. My body feels numb as I remembered my training. Thinking to myself, "Was this all for nothing?" I felt numbness consuming me. My body started to feel like ice. The three now being one said,

"You're nothing but a mutt. Your father will lose another kid today. You and your sister will die."

They started laughing and squeezing me harder and harder. I felt true disparity thinking about my sister and how if I die she does too. I just focused on my breathing blocking everything else out.

As I focused I felt something boiling from inside of me. Like a volcano starting its eruption, my body started to amass big strong muscles and I grew two feet in height. I was now seven foot tall.

"Don't tell me he just awakened his enlightenment. This fucking MUTTTTTTT!!!!!"

As I transformed their hold on me was broken. My body started to quickly regenerate. I stared at them and declared,

"You will die for jumping my sister!"

I lunged forward as they were making a response. Moving so quick they were still talking as I punched him in the stomach with the spikes created on my brass knuckles by my enlightenment.

"How many more of The Risen are out here in this forest?" I asked expecting an answer.

"None of your business you fucking mutt! You'll

be dead soon!"

They coughed up blood holding on to their stomach. He started to collapse, but I grabbed him by his head before he hit the ground.

"No, no. Don't go to sleep just yet. You threatened me and my sister. Feel this suffering a little longer."

I pushed my fist inside their chest. Deeper and deeper.

"Do you feel that? That's your heart that I am holding. I am about to rip it out! Just how you ripped out my dreams for love!"

I'm not going to lie; …I felt addicted to my new power. I started laughing seeing them so hopeless.

"Y'all died to A FUCKING MUTT!!"

Then I ripped their heart out and crushed it right before their face. I calmly said,

"You were so confident you would kill us. Now

you're going to die. Just like you should."

Their body started to collapse in slow motion it seemed. I watched it hit the ground. Their blood covered the area. I walked over to the cave and moved a huge boulder in front of the entrance. I started to feel lightheaded and collapsed on the ground.

"I did it dad. I hope you're proud of me." I muttered just prior passing out.

(...Back home in human territory.)

I felt like something was off.

"Ryan, I hope you and Zaya are safe. Please be safe I beg."

----------- Chapter 5 -----------

"Dreams"

Zaya was in a "coma like" state.

"It is so peaceful here Grandma. So warm and peaceful." Zaya whispered.

"I know baby. This is where I live now."

"And where is this?"

"Don't worry about it my little ZaZa. (nickname)"

"Baby, you're not supposed to be here yet. Ryan needs you."

" What do you mean?" Zaya asked in a whisper.

"Go to him now. I love you my little ZaZa."

I woke up seeing my brother passed out. I don't remember what happened. What's going on? Where are we? What happened? My whole body is aching. I looked over at Ryan. He's breathing, but barely. What happened to him? There is blood all over his hands and body. It looks as if he gotten taller, but I can't really tell right now. I don't know how long we've been in here, but I am starving. I saw a boulder blocking the exit. I tried to generate some enlightenment in my body, but I couldn't. So we were stuck in here. My only hope for us was to explore this cave. I rubbed my brother's forehead,

"I will return. I promise."

I headed off. Well, hobbled off. I slowly gained energy to walk. I heard water falling in the distance. I need to find that as soon as possible. I don't know how long we've been knocked out cold, but we need to stay hydrated. I know we also needed some food. I kept following the sound of the water falling in the distance. The cave barely had light so I used my enlightenment to light up my fist. I'm glad it worked this time. Getting closer and closer to the sound, I finally found the water pouring in. I grabbed some in my hands and used my enlightenment to purify the water. I drunk the water until my thirst was quenched, and had put some in my container I had in my backpack.

Now it's time to find food. Either vegetation or I will have to kill something. I walked as slow as possible not to scare off any animals. I was looking and listening out for potential food. I found one, but there wasn't a chance of hope. This animal is very dangerous. It's a Zigor. A Zigor is a polar bear that was mixed with a silverback gorilla. These came about through experiments. This was one of the new species that were introduced to our planet. I am horrified and not sure of what to do next. I can literally feel fear running through my body. Thinking about it, this animal must have scared off any other ones or ate them. So I have to kill it or be killed. I formed my staff in my hand and placed my backpack down. Thinking of what should be my next move, I took a silent deep breath. Clearing my mind, I focused on the victory we needed right now.

It's us or him. Either way one of us will die. I snuck up behind a big rock inching along. I could smell the death that lingered around. Seeing piles of skeletons, I thought to myself, "Is this really a great idea?" I sat there for a second waiting for an opening. As I inhaled I cleared my mind. My heartbeat increased and adrenalin ran through me as I planned my attack. The ground cracked under my feet as I jumped forward. The Zigor turned in an instant roaring at the top of its lungs. I hit it sending it flying into a rock wall formation. BLAM!!! The area vibrated on impact. It was enraged now standing upon its back two legs. It was at least fifteen feet tall. Probably weighing 1600lbs.

"I will take you down. We must survive."

I don't know why I'm talking to it. Maybe I'm feeling guilt. It started rushing me. I dodged the first swing; barely. If one of these connects I will die. I will have to kill this quickly or I will die. I had to end this asap. I have to make my next hit my last. I was dodging it trying to bite off my head. I vaulted backwards creating a big amount of space. I made my enlightenment into a sword-like form on the end of my staff. I started charging at it gaining speed. I could feel the amount of enlightenment increase. I could feel it sharpen at the end of my staff. In striking distance I dodged the Zigors powerful concentrated attacks. I was very patient as I moved, ducked, sidestepped, and evaded its deadly sharp claws. I was in sync with my enlightenment. I followed its flow perfectly. Thanks dad. I finally had my opportunity. I swung as hard as I could. Schwing!!! Clean thru its thick fury neck. Its opened mouth head hung in the air as its blood went all over me. Globs of spit from its sharp teeth and jaws narrowly missed me as it plopped on the forest ground. Now that it's over I felt so bad about everything I did.

I ran enlightenment throughout my entire body to strengthen me so I could drag the Zigors flesh back to my brother. There was a trail of blood that followed me all the way back to my brother. I skinned the Zigor and cleaned it. I made a fire with the sticks and dead leaves laying around us. I used the Zigors fir skin as a bed and blanket for us to sleep on. As soon as I was finished, I checked on Ryan. He was alive and his breathing improved. I sat down and started cutting a small section of the Zigor meat off. It was tough. I cooked and ate some.

"Ryan, wakey wakey."

I flicked some water on his face. He jumped up forming the brass knuckles on his hands. Fear was all over his face.

"Calm down Ryan. It's me Zaya."

He started crying and ran to hug me.

(hugging) "What happened? Why are you crying?" Zaya said confused as she looked at him with a caring smile.

"I thought you were dead Zaya. You got ambushed

by three of The Risen scouts. When I found you they were stomping you. I killed them all. I made them pay."

He hugged me again crying out the words. He was crying so hard.

"I am so sorry Ryan. I didn't know. I am so sorry."

Zaya started crying and hugged him harder.

We both sat there crying for what felt like an eternity. After we cried together, I explained what happened while he slept.

"I killed a Zigor so we can eat. I also found some water. We need a plan before we leave this cave. But for now let's eat."

He ate some of the Zigor meat. He told me how

he unlocked his enlightenment and got stronger. Plus he told me how everyone in our class is dead. We decided to sleep here for the night. We had four days left and we must get back to dad.

----------- Chapter 6 -----------

"Time"

The week is almost over. I hope my children are okay. They have two days left. I cannot wait to hear their stories. The wind picked up and two leaves blew into the window. Be okay my children.

"Hey Ryan. Do you think we have enough food left to survive?"

"Maybe. I guess we need to go hunting and head back to the meetup spot." Ryan replied.

"You're right." Zaya casually says.

We prepared to leave the cave. We both recovered a little from our injuries. Just enough that it was not a big deal to us. We were unaware we needed major medical treatment. Our Dad told us he made enemies with all three alien nations and that we will have to deal with what he had done. His sins will affect us. Me, being my father's only son, I was prepared to take on the sins and demons of my father. I was prepared to put fear into all of my father's enemies, and ready for my father's legacy to live through me.

After moving the boulder out of the way, we carefully walked out of the cave. We knew it would take the remaining days to get back to the meetup spot. I started thinking to myself again. Me and my sister will carry on what our parents have built. We will make it our own. We will......

Craaccckkkkk BOOOOOMMMMM!!!!

A Risen captain descended from the sky. Anger and blood lust covered him. His aura was death itself.

"What do we have here?"

He spoke in a very demonic voice.

"Are these the children of the famous 5? Don't even try to lie. I received a transmission from my scouts about you two."

He started walking toward us. We had nothing but fear in us now. We had hope, but in his presence it escaped us. We may have thought we might survive, and we thought we had a future, but at this moment all we thought was DEATH!

"I didn't know I was a cat."

He scoffed.

"Say something boy! You are the one who killed my soldiers! You held their heart in their face and crushed it! Now I came to do the same!"

Rage filled his eyes. While he talked Ryan balled my fist up. This is a signal that we made between us. Just in case we're faced in a situation where we cannot talk. We focused on our enlightenment. Ryan started talking trying to distract him.

"I killed them. They ambushed my sister! Beating her near death! I crushed their heart in their eyes to let them feel death. If you're going to make me suffer for what I've done..., then I have no regrets. I am happy I made them watch their heart get crushed. It... felt... great!"

A tear fell from the Risen Captain's eye.

"One of them was my son."

He paused after speaking then spoke again.

"Even if we are warriors, one of them was my son. My only son. You enjoyed killing my only child. Huh? Well good. That's why I am here. To make you feel pain just like my only child. You will die today. YOU... WILL... DIE!"

A moment of silence went by as we stared at each other. We formed our weapons. You could see the enlightenment running throughout our whole body. I knew the only thing that was on both of our minds was a teaching by our dad, "Protect each other with your life. One day I will die. One day your mother will die. You will have each other. Be family." In this moment we are our family. We must survive. In this moment we must live.

The Risen captain bulked up and two trees near him exploded from the power released. He disappeared from our eyes and the breeze stopped. We instantly went back to back. I could feel my heart racing again, but this time no fear. Just the race of knowing this might be my last fight. Knowing I might not go home. Knowing that our dad is waiting for us and he may never see our smile again.

"Ryan watch my back."

"I got you Zaya"

"I love you Ryan."

"I love you Zaya."

The forest was completely silent. Not one animal or bug was making a noise. The sky was clear. I could feel the heat of the sun burning my skin. We began to see the shadow of the Risen captain moving rapidly around us, but we didn't see him. Boom!!! Another tree exploded.

"Do y'all feel fear? To know you're going to die!"

He shouted.

I saw this giant figure appear right over us. Both his arms were cocked back. He planned on punching us both from above. We leaped and separated causing him to miss us. A crater formed as the air picked up a huge dust cloud. We were separated and that's exactly what he wanted.

"Zaya watch behind you!!!!"

Ryan shouted at the top of his lungs giving away his location on purpose. Hoping to get The Risen captain's attention, but this was unsuccessful. I turned barely blocking his horrendous fist. My staff was trembling under the pressure. Ryan ran over jump kicking him in the face. The Risen Captain smiled as if it had no effect, but we saw blood on his face. We saw it run down. Ryan swung his fist, but before he could land the punch, the Captain hit Ryan with a three punch combo sending him flying. He turned and flicked me in the forehead. My body flew backwards and I was wedged into the ground. Before he chased my brother, he did a jumping handstand and kneed me in my stomach. He turned to face me saying,

"I'll kill you later. Don't die."

He disappeared from my sight as I threw up breakfast and barely able to breathe.

"Ryan, please don't die."

I tried to yell, but I passed out.

I could see the Captain flying towards me. My only prayer is that Zaya is still alive and breathing. Please don't be dead. I smashed through a couple of trees. Blam! My body smacked against this huge tree. The Risen Captain was closing in. I must stand, but my body was hurting. I still haven't fully recovered from the previous fight. Kaboom!!!! He kicked me in my face pushing my head into a tree. His boot held me down.

"You'll know what you did to my child. My son.

My only son. You will suffer before you die today."

The Captain declared boldly.

I couldn't think anymore. This is it. I am about to die. I could feel myself fading away. I wasn't strong enough. I wasn't strong enough to live. I hope my sister runaway. I need her to live.

....

....

....

I could literally hear my skull beginning to crush...

....

I screamed in pain!

....

Ughhhhhh! So this is how I die to the boot of a Risen Captain crushing my head.

....

....

Splash!!! His body had been disintegrated. A bright green beam shot through him. His blood covered me.

"What happened? How did he die?"

I thought to myself as a random figure stood over me.

"I could not let you die here. Not like this."

----------- Chapter 7 ------------

"Lost Bonds"

"Who are you?" Ryan asked being on his side with his head up not having enough strength to stand. Zaya limped up into my view as the stranger shared.

"I am the forgotten one. I have been here for years saving kids. Or at least trying to. I don't exactly know where I come from, but I will unite you with your classmate that I could save."

I couldn't force myself to keep my head up any longer. I was exhausted yet grateful to be alive and happy the stranger saved one of our classmates. I passed out. The stranger took us to a safe place so we could rest and recover.

One day has passed since we were almost beaten to death. When we were finally awake, there was food already set for us. As we were eating,

Zaya suddenly sees the girl that Ryan liked and asked her how she survived. She was hesitant to answer. When Ryan saw her, he was automatically drawn to her like glue. His face was full of relief. Barely able to move, he started talking to his sister just for a minute when he passed out again.

The girl I like, her number is 325. When I woke up this time, she was standing over me. My number is 455. We talked probably once, maybe twice, throughout this year so I wouldn't be distracted during the exam. So this made me nervous having her standing over me like this. Her face had a slight tone of red. She smiled with tears in her eyes. Making me wonder, why does she care so much? She hugged me and started talking in a shaky voice,

"I… am so… happy you… finally woke up. 455, I was so… worried about you. I thought you… and your sister… were both killed. I was… really worried. All the rest… of our class… is dead."

Ryan replied, "You were worried about me? I was

worried about you too. I wanted to ask you your name 325." I didn't even realize I ignored she said everyone is dead, but I kind of already accepted it a week ago.

"My name is Emily, but my family calls me Lily. I have been wanting you to ask for so long. What is your name?"

Her face was now a bright red.

"My name is Ryan. I have been wanting to ask you for so long."

I could feel myself blushing.

Zaya walked near us. She was using something as a crutch. Limping still she was standing right beside them. Ryan looked up worried asking,

"Zaya, are you okay?"

"Yes, I am okay. My whole body is sore and I can't wait to get home. What happened?

Did you kill the Risen Captain?" Zaya asked.

There was a moment of disbelief as we sat there.

"No..., somebody else did. I saw a bright green beam and the captain exploded. I passed out right after."

Lily responds,

"Some guy saved me. I was being chased by a pack of sandwolves. He grabbed me and we hid. He reminded me of you and your dad."

We didn't believe her. You could see it in both of our faces. However, that did remind me of what The Risen Captain said. Lily could sense we didn't believe her.

"He did remind me of your dad Zaya and Ryan. I'm not lying."

Zaya was knocked out and didn't really know

what happened. So she was confused and was trying to have hope that other people were still alive. Maybe those bastards were lying. So she asked,

"Ryan and Lily, are there any other people alive?"

"Sadly Zaya, everyone else is dead." Ryan said looking disturbed.

We all had blank faces. After realizing everybody we grew up with was gone, we kept feeling like we were on the brink of death. One more day. We have no more food and badly injured. We were extremely exhausted. Zaya proceeded to talk.

"We will stay here for the night and head to the rendezvous spot in the morning."

We all fell into a deep slumber. When we woke up we headed out limping towards the meetup spot. We suddenly felt huge amounts of air swooshing down upon us.

"All aboard... where is everyone?"

We froze for a moment then limped onto the Zoro. After getting secured, we just sat there for a second. We all looked around and said together, "Dead." Our instructors face went from joy to sadness. As we flew off, I was looking down and thought I saw dad.

"Hey Ryan, is that dad down there?" Zaya said happily.

"No, your dad is waiting for the both of y'all at home." The instructor added.

"I really thought I saw dad down there."

Zaya says out loud to herself.

The ride back was the complete opposite of the ride there. It went from laughter and excitement to being quiet and silent. We kept our promise to our dad, but the only person to survive other than us was Lily. I couldn't think about what was going on. I couldn't feel my legs like I used to anymore. Ryan was passed out and so was Lily. When we finally returned, the group of parents there were all destroyed finding out their children were dead. It completely broke them. That day was the day I realized life isn't fair. It's not the fairytale I thought. It was not going to be easy. Lily's mom was as happy as our dad holding her tightly.

"Hey, are you okay? My children?" 5 asked. As we were walking up to our dad our sadness slowly drained from us. We ran over to him as best as we could.

"Dad, this was the worse exam we could have possibly done."

Ryan laughs a little, but quickly stops because of the pain.

"I thought we were going to die so many times dad."

Zaya started crying. Hugging me with her face on my chest she was releasing all of her pain.

"You're okay now. We are going home now. Mom is waiting for y'all." Dad noticed his son was taller, but didn't bother asking seeing their condition.

---------- Chapter 8 ------------

"Old To Present"

"We love you dad."

We headed home. We have ways of healing ourselves using special secret techniques mom was taught. Everything starting getting darker and my body started getting cold. I guess Ryan was feeling the same. We both passed out. We woke up in the ER. Come to find out we both will have to be in the hospital for some weeks. Zaya had six broken ribs and a broken leg. She will need surgery on her ribs. It will be up to five weeks before she's healed. Ryan had four fractured ribs. His skull was extremely pushed to the limit. He will need surgery and we do not know if he will make it out alive.

This left 5 in extreme sorrow. What did they have to endure? They told me what happened. It's all my fault. Being a spy who killed multiple leaders, I have a lot of enemies just like my husband. The thoughts running through my head wouldn't stop. They paid for my sins. They paid for the sins of their father. I'm supposed to be a guide. A light in the darkness. They're the future. I need to fix this. I need to end this war. I need to do this before I lose my children; ...like I lost Zero.

5 proceeded to leave the hospital going home to his wife. She was waiting patiently. Her face turned almost as if she knew what happened.

"5, what is going on? How are our children?"

She said in a concerned voice.

Freya my love, you have finally returned. I walked over and hugged her.

"They are both in deep sleep and will need surgery."

She started crying and I started crying as we began to embrace. I went on to tell her what they told me. How they fought a Risen Captain. We decided to go to the hospital taking turns staying. We both would sleep there holding each other as we waited outside of their rooms for weeks. We waited for them to heal.

"Mom and dad, how are you?" Zaya smiles.

She finally woke up.

"We are good. We been waiting for you to wake up. Ryan is still sleeping. He is right over there."

Freya said smiling. Zaya looks over,

"Is he okay?" she asked.

"No, he isn't. We will have to see if he pulls through or not. Get some rest Zaza, we love you."

Freya leans over and kissed Zaya on her forehead. Zaya leaned back and fell back into a deep sleep. The doctor said that she woke up earlier than expected and she might sleep a couple of more weeks.

Three more weeks have passed and Lily has been visiting. She has been worried about Ryan.

"Ugh…, what happened?"

Ryan says as he finally wakes up.

"5 and Freya are both gone at the moment." Lily says.

"Ryan, you finally woke up." Zaya happily smiled.

"What do you mean Zaya? What happened? Where are we?" Ryan was puzzled.

"The hospital. We both had surgery performed on us while we were passed out. Dad and mom have been sleeping outside for weeks. Apparently we were in serious condition and barely made it through. Dad and mom should be coming back in about an hour." Zaya explained.

"Good, I gotta ask them something. Remember the Risen Captain we fought?"

"Yeah, I remember. The one you beat."

"No, I didn't beat him. Remember? We talked about this. It was a random guy. He looked like dad. I got a good look at his face before I passed out." Ryan said a bit confused.

"What are you insisting? Dad was the one who saved us?"

"No! We might have an older brother or uncle that we didn't know about."

"Impossible! They would never hide that from us. We are the only family we got. Remember? We're all we got."

"We will see them tomorrow since they didn't make it back for visitation hours."

"We will ask them tomorrow. They will not come today because they had a council meeting today."

(…Meanwhile at the meeting.)

The headmaster is about to talk.

"We can't keep doing these exams. We are losing a lot of kids every year. It's not getting any better. They are our future and we keep letting them down.

All in favor of canceling this exam. Say I."

"I."

Everyone agreed. Most of the council lost their children in the last three exams.

Freya started talking to me right after the meeting was over.

"Baby, we are blessed our kids survived. 5, do you hear me? We didn't lose our kids this time."

My mind went blank. All those kids. Their smiles. Their dreams. Their ambitions. All gone. My anger was growing.

"I will end this war." I said under my breath.

Freya heard me and smiled. We kissed and went home.

"We will end this war." Freya said as we left the building.

The next day rolled around and we went to see our

children.

"Ryan you're finally awake. Zaya told us everything. You're taller. You can use your enlightenment completely now. That you got super strong, defeated scouts, and a Risen Captain. We are so happy to see you up."

Freya ran over to hug Ryan. He looked disturbed again.

"I didn't kill the Captain. I was about to die, but a man saved me. He looked like dad!"

A blank expression came over both of our parents faces. Zaya needing clarity says.

"Tell him he was just seeing things. Y'all wouldn't keep a secret like that from us. We're family. We don't hide things from each other."

Our parents looked at each other with tears

running from their eyes. Dad curiously asked Ryan.

"Are… you… sure…, son?"

"Yes! He looked just like you dad!" Ryan answered with all certainty.

A peaceful smile covered 5's face through his tears. Freya also started smiling as they cried tears of joy together. The relief was written all over their faces. They both took a deep breath almost simultaneously.

"Don't be disappointed in your parents. We kept this secret from y'all long enough. We think that was your older brother who saved you. He took the exam years ago. We thought he died, but obviously he didn't. We kept it a secret from you because we didn't want y'all to fear the exam. We didn't want y'all to be afraid to live on knowing your brother died." 5 shared while holding Freya's hands.

"Dad you should've told us. He saved my life! He saved our lives! We could've brought him home. He could have come home with us."

"We love y'all, but we need some time for ourselves." Zaya states strongly. 5 and Freya leaves the hospital room looking sad. Zaya looked out the window crying. I couldn't look mom and dad in the eyes after hearing we had an older brother. What have we done? We left our family behind.

----------- Chapter 9 -----------

"Broken Memory"

How can we trust our parents? How can we get past this? This is our flesh, our blood, that saved us. We could've done something. We didn't even bring him home.

"Zaya, did you even get to see to him?"

"Ryan, I got a good look as we flew off. He looked exactly like dad." Zaya released with excitement all over her face.

"I saw him before I passed out. He really looks like dad. Why didn't he come back yet?" Ryan's head dropped in disappointment.

"Dad just said they thought he was dead. I guess he didn't make it back to the meetup point in time."

"Maybe you're right, but you know what? I just wanna get to know him now." Ryan said as he turned over to get some sleep.

The next day was clear as the sun started rising and the birds were singing. The nurse came in bringing us breakfast. We ate our food and packed. We were released to leave today.

"How do we talk to mom and dad about this?"

Zaya looked over and waited for Ryan to answer. They both took a deep breath.

"We don't. It's just that simple." Ryan said.

We looked at each other with hurt in our eyes. They told us our family was everything. He been there for years now. Nobody, and I mean nobody, found him. Test after test. Why didn't he come back?

"WE'RE GOING TO GET HIM!"

We both shouted this at the same time.

(...Somewhere in the forest years ago.)

Everyone was killed! I mean everyone! But how

did I survive? Where am I? Am I dead? Zero was covered in blood after his clan was eaten by the trolls. He fought hard and barely escaped. He just sat there with a blank expression.

With so many questions and no answers, I fell asleep. When I woke up I thought I would be at home. That my classmates that were killed were still here. That they were still alive, but sadly no. I woke up on the cold hard rock that I put under my head. Bugs were crawling on my skin. The warmth was my imagination trying to confront the horrible things I had seen. Trolls were everywhere. They called this test, "THE DEATH GAMES," a rite of passage that we must honor. The Troll I managed to kill said this to me before dying. I watched the remaining Trolls eat my dead classmates remains. I hid until they left.

They take us for a joke. I will not let anyone else die. I will train and kill everyone who comes against our clan. I trained my enlightenment. Now

I used my blasters inside my arms. I used my blasters to hunt. I will not let no one else die. This was my only motivation. That's the only thing going through my head. I wanted to go home, but I fell asleep on the ride over here. I missed the information I should have received. My dad told me to stop being over confident, but I didn't listen. I... did... not... Listen! I should have paid attention to my dad, and my instructor. No one lived to give me the info I missed from our instructor. I didn't know what to do or where to go. It all happened so fast. Now I am alone.

Next year rolled around. I fought as hard as I could. This time the Invitca attacked. They were too fast and I almost died. I was only strong enough to save myself.

MYSELF... only me.

Again.

I was all alone.

AGAIN!

Year after year I watched my clan, my family, MY PEOPLE, take their final breath. Year after year until I finally lost who I was. Who am I truly? What was my name? I lost sense of who I am. I watched too many people die to be whoever I was before. To go back to wherever I was I couldn't remember if I tried. When this year rolled around I tried my hardest, but only managed to save one girl. She called me number 5. I did recall I was number 12, I think, but she realized I wasn't that student. I questioned myself as if that was my number. "Maybe I am 5." I thought to myself.

"You look just like somebody dad who's here. Who are you?" Emily asked.

"If only I could remember. It doesn't matter who I am. Just you getting back home." I responded.

"I have to wait a week, until then, can I stay with you?" Emily suggested.

"Then I will protect you little one." Zero says.

"Finally, I'll be able to protect someone." Zero thought to himself.

"Did you see anybody else? Is anybody else alive? Emily asked.

"No, they are not. They're dead. I will protect you though."

Zero's smile went away after saying this. The rest of them were brutally killed like so many before. Blood covers everything. This forest is covered in innocent blood.

"They will be here to get me soon sir." Emily stated.

I said nothing. I do not need her caring about me. I protected her as best as I could until I heard screaming. I picked her up and carried her to a safe place.

"Stay here until I return." She shook her head to

indicate that she understood.

When I arrived, the two that were fighting The Risen Captain were still alive. Still breathing. There was still hope. The girl was lying in a crater and The Risen captain's boot was on the boy's head. There was no time to waste. I blasted The Risen captain disintegrating his body. He never saw it coming. All that was left of him was his radio that somehow survived my blast. I picked up the radio and said,

"I hope you all back at base hear me. I'm sure y'all can hear me through his mic. If you come back here again, I WILL KILL YOU!"

I destroyed the radio and walked over to see what condition the boy was in. I was glad he was still alive. I said to him,

"I could not let you die here. Not like this."

The boy looks like someone I used to know. The girl also. They gave me a familiar feeling as if I knew them. He passed out so I carried him and the girl with him followed me limping. She passed out in route. I had to carry them both to the girl I saved. The girl I saved cried as soon as I laid them down. Tears ran down her face.

"Are they still alive?" Emily asked.

"Barely. Y'all will be home soon, right? They can get help there. I will go get food for you all."

I left them to gather food.

When I returned with food they were no longer at my safe place. They left. I placed the food down and went looking for the three of them. I was prepared to fight for them again if they were still alive. I was hoping I wouldn't find them dead. Knowing they were supposed to be picked up, I went to their meetup spot Emily shared. I arrived just as they were taking off. Once again I had that familiar feeling looking at the boy and girl. I was happy they weren't dead. I noticed the girl looked at me as I looked at her. At least I knew they would live. I disappeared into the shadows. Preparing for next years fight. I finally saved people of my clan. I felt lonely, but accomplished. However, I think I lost myself in the process. Why did those two kids remind me of a warm place? Who am I? I slowly went to sleep wondering who I was.

---------- Chapter 10 ----------

"Healing Chains"

"Zaya and Ryan haven't been speaking to us honey."

Freya said as she kissed me. We were laying in our bed.

"I know honey, but it's okay. My love, we will be better. Our family will be repaired. We will heal."

5 responded hugging her and rolling over.

"I know, but we need to go find Zero soon." Freya leaned in.

"I know baby." 5 said before kissing Freya.

We both sat up wondering why the kids weren't up yet. They're usually making breakfast or some kind of noise by now. We got up and started searching the house. Not finding the kids we became rattled...
(...Meanwhile, Ryan and Zaya)

Ryan and Zaya snuck out early this morning. We grabbed a baby Zoro and took flight.

"We must find Zero." Zaya says after waking me up.

"I know Zaya. He saved us." I said determined to bring him home.

We arrived and hovered over the forest where we had been picked up. The forest was alive with the hearing of bugs and animals. The damage that happened to the area wasn't completely healed. Broken trees and craters were everywhere. I had flashbacks of being kicked through the trees. I relived the whole experience. I was instantly drenched in sweat. My body shivering. Shaking so bad Zaya had to slap me. Smack!

"Are you okay?" Zaya asked. "Do you have PTSD?"

"I think I do. I am terrified to be honest." My voice was very shaky.

We descended to the ground and set the rules.

1. No yelling. Only talk when next to each other.

2. We have three flares. The Green one is used if we find Zero. Yellow if we're being chased and need help. Red if we can't find him, or if we do and he's dead.

3. Avoid danger at all costs.

4. We will meet here tonight and leave tonight, and come back tomorrow until we find him.

We agreed on these rules, gave our baby Zoro some commands, and began searching. We left trails of string. Different colors so we know who string it is. We split up to cover more ground. We hugged each other before separating.

"You are my family. I love you. Let's go get the rest of our family." Zaya smiled.

"I love you to Zaya. We will bring him back home." A huge smile covered Ryan's face.

We split up and journeyed off.

(...Back home.)

Hours have passed by. Freya dropped the food plates she made for them.

"Honey, where are Ryan and Zaya? My babies." Freya said in a worried manner.

"I don't know baby." 5 said nonchalantly.

"I'm worried. They haven't been speaking to us. They were gone in the morning. I think they went to get Zero."

"Get your gear my Queen. It too dangerous there.

We got to go now."

We got aboard our Zoro and left. We found their baby Zoro and found these strings.

"Which one?" Freya said holding them both.

"Freya. You take the blue one. I'll take the pink one."

"Okay baby, we got this."

We followed the strings eventually catching up to them. 5 was with Zaya. Freya was with Ryan.

"What were you thinking? Huh Zaya? Either one of you could've been hurt. It already happened once. What is your problem!? Huh!?" 5 shouted.

"Dad, my problem... no, our problem. No, what is y'all problem? Knowing we had an older brother is one thing, but leaving him is another. Why didn't y'all come back? Why did y'all leave him stranded?"

I could see the tears in her eyes and heard the pain in her voice.

"Your mother and I didn't know what to do. We've been hurting for so long. We just didn't want y'all to hurt as much as we did, but I guessed we failed at that too, huh?" We both sat down for a second.

(Somewhere else in the forest.)

Freya caught up to Ryan, but Ryan kept walking. Instead of talking they both continued to search. After a while we finally met up with the others. We looked for three days and three nights finding no trails. We finally found something. Blood. We followed a trail of it, and the trail led us to finding Zero half dead. He was passed out with a bunch of The Risen dead around him.

"Is he dead?" Freya asked. Tears rolling down all of our eyes.

"Zero... NO, NOT MY BABY AGAIN!!!!" Freya shouted out loud.

Dad and mom ran over to him. Freya took out a healing orb putting it onto his forehead. He took in a deep breath shortly after coming back to us.

The damage he took wasn't as bad as the damage the Risen took. He was waking up slowly. It was good to see him opening his eyes.

"We have been looking for you for three days."

Zaya says. Everyone was smiling but Zero.

"Who are y'all?" Zero asked.

He was soaked in the blood of the Risen bodies which were lying near him. Freya started cleaning his face off.

"I am your mother. This is your father. These are your siblings. You saved them." Freya shared in a tender motherly tone.

"I don't remember. I have been trying to protect any human that comes through these parts and been failing. I have been failing for so long." Zero said calmly.

Everyone was motionless in silence while staring at Zero. The silence was broken with a large deep cry. Zero started crying so hard that his face was being cleared of the remaining blood.

"Y'all..., where have y'all been? If you knew me, why didn't you come get me? Why did I have to see so many die?" Zero's head dropped in sadness.

5, being his father and going through something similar, heart instantly broke hearing Zero. My heart was torn to pieces. I grabbed him and embraced him. While hugging him he cried into my chest.

"I am so sorry son. So sorry. I should've searched from the top of the mountains until the very bottom of this forest. We couldn't find traces of you and gave up."

My mother walked over and hugged them both.

"I don't know y'all. I don't even know who I am. I don't remember saving those kids over there. What am I supposed to do?" Zero was barely able to let those words out.

"Come back with us. We'll show you who you are. If you don't wanna stay, we will bring you back. If that's what you want." Freya said looking at 5.

After this we sat there for ten minutes in silence. Zero finally answered.

"I will go back with you all for now. I want to know who I am."

At this moment we all shared his pain. We all cried and clearly understood his heartbreak. We walked in silence on our way to leave this forest of death. Death had a new meaning now that Zero was alive without memories. We boarded our Zoros and headed home; our new home. In the air we looked down upon the forest. This forest doesn't know this world is full of pain that we must survive.

---------- Chapter 11 ----------

"Nightmares"

Lighting cracked across the sky like bones breaking on impact. It was raining extremely bad. The thunder roared viscously. We were drenched as we hopped off the back of the Zoros. Quickly we rushed inside. Sounded like maracas were hitting the window. Zero was unusually calm. Even as we ate our dinner his expression was unreadable. Our parents disappeared into their bedroom. We tried to make small talk, but Zero still had his reservations toward us. We didn't quite know why, but I guess being in the forest would have this effect on anyone. When our parents returned, I could just make out a book tucked underneath our mother's arm. A book of memories.

"Where was this hidden?" Zaya asked followed by Ryan.

"We thought it would be best if we kept this book

to ourselves. You all were way too young to understand it all."

Freya uttered very softly. The guilt peaked in her voice. My dad just looked away in shame as his arm draped over her shoulder.

Mom slowly placed the book down on the old wooden table. Her eyes never left us. Zero's face twisted. He was visibly uneasy. How could they have gone on like this never happened? Like they weren't harboring a deep secret? Zero waited a moment before gazing at all that was inside.

"Is this me?" Zero asked.

They silently nodded their heads still gripping onto each other for moral support. He continued his gazing with tears rolling down his face. They hugged him, but even I could see his body stiffen. Ryan and I had been sitting quietly watching it all unfold before our eyes. Tears began with our parents. Zero seeing their tears eyes welled up. As tears fell from Zero, we began to tear up. While we all shed our tears, we all embraced each other in a group. Now we're a complete family with no secrets. As the day came to an end and all the secrets were on display, we were tired enough to prepare for bed. All of our emotions were raw and surreal. Zero and I (Zaya) shared a brief glance before he disappeared into the guest bedroom.

I myself haven't been dreaming at all lately, but tonight was different. As we laid our bodies down for rest, we were unprepared for the distress that would engulf us. This would be a terrible night for everyone. We all had nightmares that woke us up in a cold sweat. One by one, we all gathered at the table in our family room. A pot of tea was sitting in the middle. As I sat down, my mother slid a cup toward me. Zero told us he never went to bed and that he was down here all night long. Ryan and I both woke up screaming at the same time. Freya and 5 then followed.

"Why are y'all up?" Dad asked us.

"I had a nightmare. Did you guys have a bad dream?" Mom asked as she adjusted her robe.

"Yeah, I had one too. Who's going first?"

"Me... I'll go first." Ryan said.

"My dream started off with me being chased. Chased by The Risen Captain. The one who tried to kill me. No matter where I hid, or even if I flew away, he would catch me. No matter how hard I fought he would beat me. He beat me til I couldn't move. Until my body was completely numb. He then stood over me and told me to feel his son's pain while he crushes my head. I would always wake up before my head would splat."

Ryan was drenched in sweat after he told us his dream. Mom slowly walked over and wrapped him in her arms.

"It's okay son. You will get stronger and overcome

this." Dad, as he patted Ryan on the back, asked, "Zaya, do you wanna go now?"

"I…, …I guess."

I took a deep breath not sure where to begin.

"My dream is more of guilt. While we were out there, Ryan was out cold. We were trapped in a cave. I had to…"

Tears started to build up as my eyes turned from ice white to dark pink.

"…kill a Zigor. It was the only thing alive in that cave. I had to kill it to survive. For me and Ryan to live. It was a mother. After I killed it, I could hear her cubs. Their cries were so loud. They never stopped looking for her. I have been having the same dream every night ever since. The baby Zigors crying over her remains."

Mom sat in between us hugging us both saying, "I guess I'll go next. You all know that I can shapeshift. Thus making me the perfect candidate to be a spy. So when I go on missions, I have nightmares of coming home finding that you all were hurt. That you've been killed because of what we are. Those are my nightmares every time I leave my family."

She hugged us harder.

"Son." Dad speaking to Zero. " Do you wanna go next?"

"No, you go on," Zero answered.

"Ok, I guess I'll go then. My nightmare is similar to your mother's. I sometimes dream that when I return, no one is here. That we've been completely wiped out. That y'all were ripped away from me. Taken from me just like my parents. That I will lose everyone I love."

Dad's whole demeanor changed. He was angry like we had never seen before. His emotions for once weren't unreadable. They were raw. They were real. He took a deep breath and calmed himself. He turned his head slowly to Zero and in return, Zero took a deep breath before he nodded his head sharing,

"My nightmare... is the same every night. It's seeing the people I tried to save die. Murdered right in front of me. Hearing their screams so vividly. For so long I've had restless sleep. To the point where I don't want to sleep. My memories won't let me. When I do sleep it's just replay after replay of the endless slaughters and the horrors I've seen. Kid after kid dying before my reach. I'm so happy I saved you two and the other girl."

"We thank you from the bottom of our heart." 5 released feeling so grateful.

"We are just so happy to find you. To have met you. To bring you back home." Ryan happily adds. We all stayed up til morning.

It was time to get ready for the Exam

Ceremony. For the ones who passed. We haven't had one of these in two years.

"Get ready you guys, come on."

Freya clapped her hands together. Boom!!! The living room exploded!!! Rubble was everywhere. Smoke and dust were in the air.

"WHERE IS 5 ?!!!!!!!!!"

---------- Chapter 12 ----------

"Vengeance"

Waking up seeing rubble everywhere, I couldn't have been out too long. My family was passed out all under the debris. Our home was almost destroyed completely. My sons, my daughter, and wife, were completely out of it.

"I AM HERE!!!"

5 shouted in fury at the top of his lungs.

Anger flowed off of me like boiling water and fueled my enlightenment which grew greater and greater. Consuming every cell in my body. I went blind only seeing him. My fixation couldn't be broken.

"I WILL DESTROY YOU!!!" I roared with every ounce of my being.

The person before me was of The Risen race. He

was a commander. A top dog. His feet never touched the ground. That was the pride of a Commander. Amongst the other races who walk, their feet are never to touch the ground.

"We need your head 5! We now know this is your son's doing! He killed many of our warriors over the years! Not just ours, but of the other alien races. His bounty is more than enough for forgiveness. But we need your head too for the humans to be forgiven. We know that the humans stand no chance!"

The Risen Commander's face did not change. He stayed composed the whole time.

"You will have to take my head from my dead body. Too bad you won't even get the chance. I'm going to make you pay. Make you wish you never existed. You FUCKED YOURSELF MESSING WITH MY FAMILY!!!"

In that instance 5 summoned his blades filling

them with enlightenment. They were the embodiment of the sun. He lunged himself straight to the commander. The commander vanishes from sight. Punching 5 in the air, you heard a loud KABOOM!!! The impact alone pushed the rest of the debris off of his family. The Risen Commander took notice of 5's family. He was about to kill them all. He started flying towards them with deadly intentions. 5 immediately flew over and swung at The Risen Commander trying to cut his head off. The Risen Commander ducked kicking 5 into the sky. After kicking 5, he headed back to 5's family. 5 had lost consciousness for a moment, but was still fueled by his anger. He swiftly recovered, focused himself, and attacked. Diving straight down, he drove his swords right into the back of the commander. The commander screamed in pain. Blood splattered everywhere. He grabbed 5 slamming him into the ground. His body hit the ground so hard it bounced up off impact. Before 5's body touched the ground a second time, the commander kicked 5 into sky then disappeared, reappearing above 5 punching him in his chest. You could see the impact to his body, but 5 stayed in the air absorbing this blow.

"Sounded like some of your ribs cracked 5. Weak humans." He scoffed and sneered.

5 focused on summoning his swords, but before he could finish he got kicked flying through a couple of buildings. The neighbors and witnesses were terrified screaming, running, and ducking for cover. The commander disappeared and reappeared floating just over 5 in the debris of the building. 5 coughed up blood and some hit the Risen Commander's face causing him to be overjoyed.

"I will not let my son die or my family. Nobody here will die today. But You!"

5 barely shouted.

His chest was pushed in. 5 put all his enlightenment

to his legs. The Risen Commander lifted his boot to crush 5's head, but 5 side-rolled, rose instantly, and ran. Increasing his speed he disappeared from the commander's eyes.

"What's going on commander? You can't see me? Too bad. I will kill you soon. But you will suffer before this." 5's voice was menacing as he sliced the commanders Achilles. 5 continued slicing him as he collapsed to the ground.

"AHHHHHHHH!!!"

The Risen Commander yelled with all of his soul.

"You thought you were going to just waltz in here and kill us."

5 sliced his back making sure not to be seen by The Risen Commander.

"You thought wrong. You thought you were going to kill me and my family today. Not today."

5 sliced through his body cutting him clean in half

top to bottom.

"I know this isn't enough to kill you. I will make you regret ever coming here."

He held both sides of his head making sure it didn't fall apart.

"Look at me in my eyes you BASTARD! If I don't crush your heart, you won't die right? Huh, Commander?!"

5 decapitates him. Both halves fell separately from his neck. He was still able to speak somehow.

"AAAAAAAAAAAAAHHHHHHHHHH, I DONT REGRET NOTHING 5! NOTHING!" The Commander yelled.

5 scoffed as he stood over his split decapitated head, and seeing The Commanders feet touch the ground pleased 5. Blood poured from his body as 5 snatched The Commander's heart out dropping it on the ground. He held the Commanders split head together under his foot and

made him watch as he took both of his blades cutting clean through his heart. The Commander died instantly.

"Wow! 5 you're so great. We tried to stop the Commander, but he overwhelmed us." The general uttered as he arrived with reinforcements right when 5 killed the Commander.

"It's okay. Just make sure we have that ceremony because my kids deserve it. They risked everything for this moment. Dammit, they will have it."

5 ran back home. His family was okay. The neighbors, and those who witnessed the destruction of their home, helped them.

"Are y'all okay?" 5 said as he drew closer to home barely able to hold his breathing.

"Yes we are. They are fine and so am I baby. Are you okay?" Freya said hugging her husband's beat up body. "I'll be just fine. I'm using my enlightenment to heal myself for now. We got to head to the ceremony." 5 said looking Freya in the eyes. They kissed, hugged, and walked to a neighbor's house.

"Can we get ready here?" Freya asked.

"You know you can 5 and Freya. Y'all are family."

We bathed and got prepared. I had to put bandages around my wounds. There are only three students graduating this year out of 50. The last two years it was 0. At least three made it this time, but I am sick and tired of all these children dying.

The ceremony started. It was very big although a few passed the rite of passage. Our Human leader was present and gave a short speech.

"We are here to show our utmost appreciation for these noble warriors who survived the exam that many did not. These three will fight for the human race. Who will put fear in those who come against us. You are our family. We will die for you. We want you to live for us."

He turned around looking at us smiling from ear to ear. Everyone stood and applauded them. All three of them cried until snot ran down from their noses.

"Come, and let us know your name." Our leader turned and signaled us to walk towards him.

Student 455 walked forward. "My name is Ryan."

They gave him his crown.

Student 273 walked forward. "My name is ZAYA!" She yelled as they gave Zaya her crown.

Student 325 walked forward. "My name is Emily." She cried as she walked forward. They gave her a crown.

Student 12 walked forward. "Zero. My name is Zero." He shed tears of happiness and joy. He was the last to be crowned.

Everyone rejoiced.

"We didn't know that Zero was alone out there fighting for his life and trying to save others. He has the most respect of this clan. You are a hero to our people and no thanks can ever repay you for your sacrifice. That's why you graduated today." The leader of the Humans paused for a second before speaking again.

"We will always welcome you all. We will always love you." Tears rolled down his face.

Fireworks sounded off. Music, dancing, and rejoicing was all that you could hear for miles. A triumphant celebratory event.

This is our family now. We will never leave you or your side.

---------- Chapter 13 ----------

"New Beginnings"

It's been about three months since the ceremony. Zaya, Ryan, and Zero have been training. They are working on how to use their powers better. To perfect them. But soon, I will test them. Their mother and I will push their skills to its breaking point and beyond.

They came running from the backyard of our new home. Our former house was small. The community built us a bigger house with a huge backyard. That's where we train.

"Dad, what is it? You have been smiling and telling us that you have a surprise at the end of the week." Ryan smiled holding his equipment.

"Ryan don't worry. You will see soon enough." 5 said smiling.

I made them rest for two days before they start their special missions. I will test them and push their limits.

"It's the end of the week dad." Zaya says happily.

Ryan and Zero followed close behind smiling.

In these three months, Zero's PTSD has gone away. He has really gotten close with the family.

"Well, let's go to the backyard you guys." Dad said.

Once in our backyard, he throws our equipment down on the ground. It was a brief moment of silence. All of them marveled at me for a second.

"Gear up." 5 smiled and started to laugh.

We all looked confused at first then we smiled. I guess he doesn't see us as kids anymore.

"Alright old man. We won't hold back." Ryan said ecstatically.

"I wouldn't want it any other way son." I said as I walked off to go change.

"So, are we doing one on ones or all at once dad?" Zero asked.

"All at once. You are strong, but not strong enough to fight me by yourselves yet." 5 stated confidently.

Mom walked up laughing hysterically.

"It's not just a one versus y'all, it's both of us versus you guys." Freya giggled.

The kids sat there surprised. They trained with dad multiple times, but mom, on the other hand, was a handful. Not knowing her tendencies was going to be a problem. We stood in the middle of our backyard. It had a lot of trees and there's a river cutting through. The wind started blowing. Swwwwwoooooooosshhhhhhh, and leaves danced in the air. No words were spoken. We smelled the food that the neighbors were barbecuing.

"I'm going to throw this ball in the air. Once it hits

the ground the match will start. The only way to win is by submitting or forfeiting." As 5 was saying this, the ball had already been tossed. It hits the ground and the ball exploded. Smoke was everywhere. Dad vanished. He punched Zaya into the distant yard area.

"Baby, you got the other two. Whoop they ass!" He laughed a hefty laugh. Cracking his knuckles, he went to fight her solo.

I stood in front of my two sons. I formed two smaller flails. I filled my body with enlightenment. They formed their weapons. Ryan making his brass knuckles and Zero's blasters opening up in his arms.

"So, no talking huh mom?" Ryan asks. She started moving forward.

I jumped towards them. Time froze for a moment. The surrounding area stood still, but they reacted just in time. The ground crumbled under the weight of my flails. I was aiming to end this in one hit. To counterattack, Zero did a full powered blast making the ground rumble below our feet. Dust was everywhere. I used this as cover to come up behind him. I transformed into Ryan. He wasn't expecting it since we haven't fought before. Using my flails I crushed Zero's arms where his blasters were located. He screamed in pain. Ryan swung at me with crushing intent. He missed me hitting and cracking the tree in two. I swept his legs. His body floated in the air. I used my other flail to smack him in the chest. I knocked the air out of him. The ground was blown to pieces. I left him in the crater. I went back to finish Zero, but he disappeared.

Zaya and dad were fighting by the river. She formed her staff. Dad had his swords out. He tried to punch her in the stomach again, but she predicted it and dodged with a counterattack. She smacked 5 right in the face. He was sent flying through a tree. He flipped and exploded off another tree behind him. Going straight to Zaya, he used his blades to knock the staff out of her hands. She let the staff disappear. She began using her hands. Right - left - up the center she swung. She was extremely fast. Faster than before. She started using kicks. Landing the last two kicks she smiled. 5 also smiled.

Zaya rushed 5. Her speed increased so fast that she was on par with her dad. As she closed in on her dad, she landed a combo, but had no power behind it. 5 connected with a right. She was not fazed by it. Forming her staff she connected 6 straight hits to the head sending her dad in the air. She jumped slamming her staff into her dad's head. KABOOM!! He was passed out. Dad did not take her seriously and let his guard down.

"I did it! I beat dad!" Zaya shouted in victory.

"Now you face me baby girl." Freya closed the distance in a heartbeat.

Zaya turned around instantly getting hit in the chest

with the flail, sending her flying into a nearby boulder. The air escaped her lungs, but she wasn't done. She stood back up. Closing the distance, she hit Freya in the stomach with her right hand. She formed her staff slamming it down on Freya's head. Freya grabbed Zaya by her arms spinning her in circles. She let her go slinging her. Her bones cracked against a tree. Freya got ready to finish her off, but Zaya passed out so Freya let her guard down. Thinking to herself, "Am I going to hard?" In a split second Zero appeared in front of her. Full blast at point blank range, he sent Freya flying. She flew into the air rolling on impact.

"I think the kids won this one." She says just before she passed out.

Zero felt bad that everyone was passed out so he went to get blankets and pillows. Joining them outside, everyone slept in the backyard that night. This day marked the day of independence as they slept in complete peace.

---------- Chapter 14 ----------

"Morning Joy"

It's the breaking of day. The sun just cracks open the sky. The sun rays oozing out like yoke from an egg. The dark purple escaped as the sun rose. Birds chirping. You could smell the dew off the grass. My face was soaked in the morning dew. We were still outside asleep. As I awakened, my body was sore, my head ringing, and I was hearing some buzzing. How long have we been out? I looked and saw my siblings laid out. Blankets covering all of us. Mom and dad were not out here.

"Hey y'all, get up. Come on. Where are our parents?" Zaya shook them as she talked.

"Let me sleep damn it." Ryan and Zero both said rolling over.

"It's okay Zaya. We went to make y'all some breakfast." Zaya turned slightly.

As Freya walked up I smelled bacon. She handed me a plate and my stomach growled. I felt my empty stomach. I could see my mom's reaction. She was giggling as she handed me my plate.

"Somebody is hungry. Eat up. Y'all are more than ready for what this world will throw at you. I am so proud of you. You beat your dad all by yourself and even help them beat me. I knew you had it in you."

She sat down beside me hugging me tightly for a second. I didn't feel comfortable with the compliment.

"I felt as if I didn't do enough." Freya said in an uneasy manner.

"What do you mean mom? I fought y'all because we worked hard. I felt weak during the exam with me and Ryan. When we got attacked by The Risen captain, I was no help. I just wanted to be strong like you and dad." Tears rolled down my face.

I felt pain in the depths of my soul. It ached just to think about it. Tears started to roll down my mother's face. She didn't say a word, but the warmth of her being here was enough. She hugged me so tight. I felt so secured and my heart warmed. I looked down at my plate and started to gorge.

"We think you're the strongest of all of us. You have always been strong my little ZaZa. Your Father and I love you so much."

Dad walked up from the back door saying,

"You are the heart of this family. You hold this family together." 5 went to wake up her siblings.

"Y'all get up now." He walked over and shook them. "Breakfast is made. Come on y'all."

Zero and Ryan got up confused.

Zero started yelling, "Y'ALL REALLY KICKED OUR ASS LIKE THAT! THEN LET US SLEEP OUTSIDE!?"

All of us started laughing.

"You know we did." Freya says to 5. They gave each other a high five before walking in the house.

"Now bring y'all asses in here and eat before I eat it all." 5 says still laughing. That morning was one of the good memories.

A couple of days went by. We started talking with the leaders about our skills. What mission we should take and how, or if, we are compatible with the mission.

"So, Ryan and Zero, what did they say y'all would be doing?" 5 asked.

Ryan answered, "Probably, a lot of front line stuff. Most of the enemies know about me and Zaya after the exam. So I will probably be a first-line defense if we get attacked. I will be a commander."

Zero answered, "They told me I would be with my mother. A spy because I am not well known. Everybody I came across that wasn't human, that tried to kill me, are dead. Nobody knows who I am. I will be training with mom to work on my shapeshifting. Then I will be going back with her to the Invitca territory."

Zaya began to speak, but paused. "With mom...,
...huh?"

Everyone became quiet.

Ryan asked, "Well, what about you?"

Zaya looks up into the sky, "I'll be like dad and go on recon missions. I will go out and get us the resources that the enemy has. Me and him make up a unit now. We will be working together."

Ryan and Zero looked super happy. The day went by and our family was full of hope and ambition. It was a great day.

Ryan and Lily have been talking a lot lately and going on dates. Zaya has been training with Zero. Mom and dad have been talking with the leaders of the human delegation. Telling them the secrets that mom learned in the Invitca territory. How they plan on taking out all the other nations soon. But for now we are safe.

Time was moving fast, but at this moment everyone had joy. A month went by. Ryan has been going to the army training grounds. Me and dad been working on our signals and formations. As well as our transformation techniques. Since some of our missions will need stealth, he was showing me the different types of forms that other races use. How to hide my scent. Time went by and our first mission is today.

Bang, bang, bang. Zaya knocked on mom and dad's bedroom door.

"Hey dad. Let's go. We got a mission today."

I got up extra early today. I knocked on his door again.

"Come on. Get up dad. Today's the day. Let's go."
Dad and mom were kissing each other goodbye and

ignoring me as they continued.

"Baby you gotta promise me you'll be safe. Don't let nothing happen to Zaya. I know you went easy on her."

5 kissed Freya again just a little longer. He started saying,

"I couldn't hurt my little Zaza, but she held her own. I will protect her with my life. You're the one who needs to be safe. They're watching you. You've got to be careful. Give Zero some tips on y'all way over there." They both rolled over and got out of bed.

Opening their door they saw the excitement on Zaya's face. Zero and mom had a mission today so Ryan will have the house to himself for a month or two. We had to get ready to leave, but we took our time eating our last breakfast together before gearing up. This will be the last meal together for awhile.

"We love you Ryan."

Each one of us told him as we hugged him goodbye as tight as we could.

"We will be back." We all stated confidently.

"Promise?" Ryan questioned his family.

"We promise." Everyone responded.

----------- Chapter 15 -----------

"Alone"

Everyone has been gone for a couple months now. I have the house to myself and it was never this quiet. I don't like this. I don't like this at all. I miss my family. On a bright note, Lily and I have been hanging out a lot. She wants to come over.

"Hey Ryannnn. How are you today?" Lily snickered.

"I'm good. Just missing my family. How about you?"

"Good. You know I'm a teacher now at the academy. I am so happy they prohibited the exams."

"They did? That's awesome. They will never know the pain of never seeing their friends again." Ryan shared as his facial expression saddened.

Both of our heads dropped remembering the events from three years ago. Lily then says,

"I heard someone's birthday is coming up."

She smiled. She came over and hugged me so tight I felt my bones pop. She continued.

"We're going to celebrate your birthday. I promise."

The eye contact was strong between them.

"Well, my birthday is tomorrow. I'm going to be fifteen. Last year we couldn't celebrate because of my injuries. My injuries training in the army."

Ryan balled his fist up looking at the scars. We both laughed then headed off to start our day. Memories of my old classmates flooded into my thoughts like a dam breaking. Their real names I never knew. The pain keeps coming back stabbing me over and over again. I wished we could've all passed the exam. I wished we could laugh together again. Lily was still with me and I don't think she caught on to me being sad.

"Well Ryan, I will see you later." Muah.

We kissed and she headed off to work.

I headed to the base. Walking down the street was like walking down memory lane. Passing the old shops that me and my friends used to go to. The old restaurants that my family would celebrate at. Walking by where our old house used to be. So much was on my mind. I needed to get ready to train. Mentally I started burying my memories again. "I have been training my ass off." I thought to myself. I was getting bigger and stronger. I was trying to move up in the rankings. I couldn't be weak anymore. I said I was going to be a commander. But right now, I am just a recruit. I must move up quickly. I must be strong enough to protect Lily. Just in case my dad isn't here next time. I want to be able to protect what's left. What remains.

The day went by and our training was intense. I was soaked in sweat. "I haven't talked to Lily all day." I thought to myself as I got ready to go home. I started walking home and got hungry. I ordered some food. When I went to pick my food up it was close to midnight. I really didn't want to be home alone. I slowly dragged myself there. Just wanting to eat and go to sleep, I unlocked my door. The house suddenly lit up.

"Surprise!!!"

Lily was standing there alone blowing a horn,

"Happy birthday!!!"

There was a projector set up where I could see all my family members faces. One by one they wished me a happy birthday.

"Happy birthday Ryan. We may not be there in person, but we're there in spirit. We love you son from the bottom of our hearts. Enjoy your night." Freya and Zero both had speeches. Lily walked over to me.

"I cooked for you. I got the whole night planned. Just for us."

Emily walked over grabbing my hand and started smiling. She led me to the kitchen. I could smell the food she cooked. My mouth was watering. The food I bought I put in the fridge. We made our plates and sat down talking about our day. She was very excited about being a teacher. How the kids were very shy, but she could help change that. After our meals, we washed the dishes and started goofing around. I couldn't help but feel joy. I hugged and picked her up twirling her around. We kissed.

"You are the best girlfriend I could ever have. I love you." Ryan stared into her soul.

Her eyes widened as he smiled.

"What did you say?"

I stopped and realized what I said. "I...." before I

could finish speaking she kissed me again.

"I love you too. Now let's enjoy the night."

(...Somewhere deep in the forest.)

Zaya and 5 set up camp for the night.

"Dad, what resources are we trying to get?"

"We are trying to retrieve the Onyx pearls. They will be a great source of money for us." Dad answered.

"But don't they reside in the troll territory?"

"Yes they do, but we are not alone. My friends Shoya and Martin will be there to back us."

"Should we call Ryan? You know today is his birthday. I know we made the video..." Zaya sounded concern.

"...No, Lily asked us for the video early wishing him a happy birthday. So we should be good. I think she threw him a party."

"You're right. Goodnight dad."

"Goodnight ZaZa. I love you baby girl."

"I love you more dad."

(...Somewhere deep in Invitca territory.)

"We have been awaiting your return Lord of Death. Who is this with you?" An Invitca official bowed before Freya.

Freya began to speak.

"This is my new recruit. He will be by my side from now on."

Freya and Zero walked into the palace. A couple of days before, Freya and Zero had to make rules.

"We will not be found out, Right mom?" Zero was extremely nervous.

"No son we won't, but you will see another side of me. You know the Invitca are ruthless. You will see the dark side that comes with being a spy."

"I have seen way worse in that forest mom. I have done way worse."

She looked at me with sadness.

"It's okay. We will overcome that soon enough. First, we do not talk about home at all. Second, you cannot depend on me. They will know something is up so you'll be on your own. Third, they are completely different. I got to let you know don't be too compassionate. Be ruthless. Be heartless."

I shook my head agreeing with her. I started thinking how things have changed in just a couple years. Everybody has started a new part of destiny. To bring the humans on top again.

---------- Chapter 16 ----------

"Lost"

Dad and I woke up and ate breakfast at the crack of dawn. We are putting on our light armor today. So that we can be agile and get in and out.

"Hey Zaza, don't be afraid. If we get caught be prepared to kill."

"Kill?..." Zaya responded looking disturbed. "...The one time I killed something I couldn't eat for a month."

"It's okay. I'm here with you. Plus, they're going to try to kill you so that should help."

We started packing up and put out the fire. Dad went to talk to Shoya and Martin.

"How's it looking y'all?"

"Good. They don't know we're here. We should be

in and out. Just like we thought." Martin said.

"Okay y'all keep watch. I, and Zaya, will go and get the Onyx pearls. Alert us if anything goes wrong." 5 started to prep.

"Copy. Y'all be safe and if anything goes wrong alert us. We will back you up." Shoya responded.

"Copy"

"Come here ZaZa. This mission is very important right now. We as a nation are starting to run out of materials. The only thing that gives us any leverage are the Onyx pearls. You will be challenged. We must stay quiet. We will use camouflage items. Turn yours on."

We both turned on our devices. Disappearing from sight. Since we both had them on we could see each other. Dad calls Shoya to make sure they were invisible. She responded that we were indeed out of sight.

"Make sure you keep your breathing low. Trolls

have extremely good hearing. The slightest noise will be picked up. Okay Zaya?"

"Okay Dad."

I started thinking to myself that this is the real deal. I felt nervous yet excited at the same time. Hoping everything goes well so I don't have to kill anyone. As we drew closer to their camp, there weren't that many Trolls. They were moving the pearls using carts. Dad told me we will only need one full cart. It will last us for the next two years, but they had about 20 carts full. The Trolls are a rich nation. These carts are nothing to them.

We separated using our quickness. We knocked out two trolls by using their only weak point against them. It's located in the back of their head right about their necks. You have to press really hard for it to work and we were not trying to kill them. We snuck up behind them not making a peep. Crack!!! You heard the spot push in and they were out cold. We grabbed the cart and started to unload. Once the bag was full we hid them in the cloak with us. We had to leave before they spotted the bodies. We slowly made our way out and met up with Shoya and Martin.

Shoya talking, "That went way better than our first retrieval mission."

Martin laughed, "It sure did. Right 5?"

My dad started laughing, "It sure did. We almost died and barely made it out."

My mind began wondering, "how many missions has my dad been on? How many people did he kill? How many times did he come back home as if nothing happened?" Over and over again, he would leave for a couple days at a time while we stayed with the neighbors. I thought back to when he would come home. A smile on his face, but tears filled his eyes. I wondered what he had done to keep us safe. To keep us alive.

Tears filled my eyes. "Dad, I love you"

"What's up with the randomness baby girl? I love you too."

"We gotta start heading back." 5 said.

It took us a month to get out there. It was going to take us a month to get back.

"ZaZa we're not going to be seeing Zero or Mom anytime soon. Okay?"

"Why not?" Zaya was confused.

"Mom is a spy you know. She is very high ranking in the Invitca army. She can shapeshift, and so can Zero. That's why he was sent with her. They call her, "The Queen of Darkness." I'm not going to lie. I don't know how this will affect Zero. This mission is very important."

"Okay. Will they be okay?" Zaya asked.

"Yeah. They should be okay. We gotta trust they will be smart. I can't afford to worry about them. I can barely sleep knowing what y'all are facing in the world now."

Worry overtook my dad's face. I should've kept my thoughts to myself. Nonetheless, we kept continuing on our journey back home.

(...Back at home.)

Ryan and Lily were making breakfast. Lily was extremely happy.

"I got my first class with a bunch of new students today. They changed the academy since we were there. Now we all know each other's names. We can actually make connections with each other. We don't have to hide our names or our identity. We can be real people." Lily says expressing joy.

I was very happy hearing the information Lily told me. I thought about all of my classmates. The names I never knew. I couldn't make real bonds. No one knew if they would make it back.

"I wanna protect all of your students. I will protect

them." Ryan said with a serious tone.

She walked over to me and we kissed.

"Now let's eat up. We got big days ahead of us." Ryan said as they both smiled and sat at the table.

After we finished eating our breakfast, we headed off in two different directions. I went to the training grounds wondering about Zaya and my dad. They said they would be home in two weeks; maybe three.

---------- Chapter 17 ----------

"Challenges"

Waking up hearing the sirens. The last couple of days I have been training my ass off. Me and mom have been in the Invitca territory.

"GET UP MAGGOTS!!! YOU WILL SERVE YOUR NATION. THE INVITCA ARMY IS THE GREATEST IN THE GALAXY. WE WILL CONQUER ALL!!!"

Thank God that mom taught me their languages. She also gave me a device that is hidden. This device helps me understand and translates to me. This huge Invitca guard stood over me. "GET UP MAGGOT!!" I rolled out of bed exhausted. We have been training nonstop. They want us to increase our speed, especially since the Invitca depends on that the most. We need to be able to avoid getting caught.

I was very exhausted, but in their rankings I am top five. I am trying to move up the ranks to at least be top three. Since mom and me won't be returning home anytime soon, I gotta move up and become stronger. When it comes to various tests, I am excelling extremely. No one can really mess with me. I haven't talked to mom since I got here. They know her as the Queen of Darkness. Here she is ruthless and shows no mercy. I honestly don't know if I recognize her. I heard she tortures people and mentally destroys them. That she makes their mind a complete mess. An egg with no yolk. She's far from the person I grew to know. She is a monster here, but she warned me. She told me I would see another side of her that I wouldn't recognize at all.

I started putting my gear on and headed out for the morning run. I had a vision last night, or dream, I can't really tell. I don't know what to do with these, but this one was different. It was horrible. Something that we could not stop if it's true. I've been having the same dreams over and over again.

We win, but at the same time we lose everything.

"MAGGOTS! Y'ALL HAVE ONE MINUTE TO FINISH FIVE MILES! SO GET TO RUNNING NOW!"

I picked up the pace and finished with ten seconds to spare. Afterwards we went to get breakfast. The food here wasn't that bad. I mean I'm used to eating stuff like this. I'm pretty sure Ryan and Zaya would hate this. I always sat alone during meals. I don't want to make any connections. No friends because one day I will have to kill them all. Everybody here must go. They only want to destroy us. Trying to prove they're the superior race.

Sadness overtook me realizing I would have to kill everyone here. That more blood was going to be on my hands. I couldn't handle it.

"Today you maggots are going to race. The loser will have to become a punching bag for the others.

Got it?" The chief in charge yelled.

Everybody answered, "Yes Sir!"

"Hey... Hey, you there. The one who came in with the Queen of Darkness. You will be with the fastest of the students. We need to see your potential. Jet, Semal, Wan, and what's your name? (He pointed to me)"

I answered, "My name is Paul."

"Paul get over here. That's a weird name. You will all be running a thirty mile race. There are obstacles and consequences in your way. You slip up and it will cost you greatly. Line up here."

We all walked over and took our stances. The other runners looked as if they had already won.

"Ready... set..... BOOM!!!!"

We took off. All I felt was the wind howling in my ear. It felt as if we floated through the terrain. Going this fast made me wanna run harder. It made me addicted to the rush. I noticed that Wan looked at me and smirked. I wondered what that smirk was for. He swung on me. I dodged it narrowly. Now I had my answer. I wasn't surprised all of them hated me. I looked around and saw they completely surrounded me.

"We will not let you win. You will be dead last if you're still alive." Wan stated.

We picked up speed as we headed down the mountain. I pulled out my blasters. Aimed it right at their head. I swiftly aimed it at the ground two steps in front of them. BOOM!!! That made two of them lose their balance causing them to stumble. Wan started trailing me and pulled out a sword. He was the fastest one in training and we had two miles left to go. He swung almost taking my head off. I turned around with one flash powered blast I let loose. He cut it completely in half. The trees around us exploded. The finish line was ten seconds away and he was gaining. We ran with all of our might. He gave up trying to hurt me and focused on winning the race. Zooommmmm!!!!! A strong gush of wind flew by as we came to a halt.

"It's a FUCKING TIE YOU MAGGOTS! So..., I guess those two back there will be the punching bags. Y'all both are safe."

We stared at each other. He looked as if he knew my real identity. Does he know me?

Later that day, when I headed to get my dinner, that group watched me the whole time. Making sure I wasn't figured out I left. Now in my bed I wondered if I've seen them before this. How would they know my shifting abilities are on par with mom's? Losing myself in my thoughts, I fell into a deep sleep.

---------- Chapter 18 ----------

"Two Lives"

We all live two lives. Right? I am a mother. A wife. Somebody's role model. I'm even a leader. But here... who I am...? I am the truth. Death to the weak. I strengthen the weak with fear. I conquer for a nation who, if they knew who I am, would have me killed. They would make an example out of me. However, that excitement was like a drug. I was hooked. That's why I show no mercy to them. I will make it home at the end of this. I will see this mission through. To see my kids. To love them the right way. The way they deserve to be loved.

I am learning this new technology they are building to wipe out the other aliens and humans. A whole race in minutes. Not just on this planet, but every race in the whole universe. That's why I am here. To learn their secrets. To know who they really are. To see the evil behind their nature. I brought my oldest with me because he is the most experienced. He can handle being on his own and continue the mission if I was to be found out and killed. I have been feeding him information in his dreams. I gave him a device to help him translate, but it also lets me put information into his mind. He will know everything I do in due time. He will know both of my separate lives.

(...Somewhere close to the human territory.)

5, Zaya, and their friends were just getting back.

"I wonder how Ryan has been doing since we left dad. He probably has gotten stronger. I might have to train with him."

"He probably did my lil ZaZa. Let's go find him."

We searched at home first. We didn't find him there. We then proceeded to walk the town. We ran into Emily.

"Have you seen Ryan Emily?" Zaya asked so causally.

I ran over and hugged her. My dad walked up behind me.

"He's training. He said he would be home later. Don't call me Emily. Just Lily." She started laughing.

My dad responded, "No, we're going to be calling you Emily from now on, okay?"

"Hey dad, I'll go find Ryan, okay?"

"Okay ZaZa. I'll go deliver these supplies."

"Okay." I headed off with joy in my heart.

(…Somewhere in the forest training.)

"I have to get stronger or everything will end. I don't know why I keep having these visions about everything we're fighting for in our lives, my family, and me. I'm seeing a place I have never been. We are crying and a bright light goes off. Everything is gone after that. "What does this mean?" Tears rolled down my face. I MUST GET

STRONGER. Ryan was exhausted and decided to go home.

"Ryan, is that you?"

Zaya ran over and hugged me tightly.

"Are you okay?" Zaya was surprised to see him back at home.

"Yeah. Don't worry about it. I am just so happy to see you. I missed y'all so much. Where is dad?"

"He went to sell the pearls. Let's train some tomorrow, okay? Let's go get some food Lil bro."

"Okay Zaya." We both proceeded to find dad. Once we found dad, he decided to grill some bbq. Today was a celebration of my first successful mission. We grilled our food and had adult drinks for the first time. We were having a joyful conversation. Ryan started talking with worry covering his face.

"Dad I had a dream..., we all died in a flash of light. I had this dream every night after my birthday."

"What do you mean son?" My dad said as he stuffed his face. I stood up near the grill.

"We died fighting. Me, you, mom, Zaza, and Zero. None of us made it out." Tears rained from his eyes hitting the grill. You could hear it sizzle and see it evaporate. His eyes became dark red and bloodshot. Like he hasn't been sleeping for awhile.

"I will never let y'all die. I will make sure you all live no matter what."

I hugged Ryan, pulled Zaya closer, and let out a hefty laugh. We shared a quiet time at home after this moment. Zaya's first mission was a success, but Zaya feels like she failed. Her brother has been having nightmares for two months now. He was alone and in pain. I guess she's not considering Emily, but she feels like she failed Ryan. When we went to bed, I watched Ryan fall asleep. Zaza slept in a chair in his room. That night I watched him for hours before I went to my own bed. Zaya was still asleep in that chair.

When we woke up in the morning, we just sat there for a second.

"No nightmares tonight, huh Ryan?" I asked still sitting the chair.

He just laid there with no response as I watched my brother closely.

I woke up thinking of my wife, my son Zero, and my children. My world I would die for. My eyes closed as I laid in my bed. Why do we have to give so much for a world that doesn't care? Everything went black. My wife appeared before me. Her face was blank, but I knew it was her.

"Baby I need you. I miss you." She started running. The kids came from out of nowhere and ran with her. Fear covered them. A light erupted from out of me. They were running from me. I woke up screaming, "Nooooooo!" What does this mean?

---------- Chapter 19 ----------

"Coming Days"

Waking up in a cold sweat, the pain completely covered my heart. Never have I felt this kind of sorrow. I thought to myself, "Did I kill them? Did I watch my family's future?" Zaza and Ryan rushed into my room. "Dad, are you okay? We heard you scream."

Zaya says as Ryan watched from a short distance.

"What are y'all doing up? Go back to bed. Everything is okay."

They left my room, and on the way out they both said, "We love you dad. We were just concerned that's all."

Morning came and breakfast was made. We just finished our morning training. No one discussed what happened yesterday. We have been trying to avoid having that talk. Mom just sent a message through.

"Hey my babies. This includes you too 5. Zero and I are making good progress. I think I'm on to something. Zero is moving up the ranks fast. I hope he is okay. I love you all. Muah." The message hangs up. We sat there in silence.

"Dad, are you really okay?" Ryan asked. We both were so concerned for our dad.

"Yes my children. I am okay. Just missing your mom and brother. I will do anything to protect y'all."

We got ready for the day while Ryan headed off to work. Zaya and I went to the council to see about our next mission.

"I already told Shoya and Martin. We will be going into The Risen territory next. Zaya, we will be doing a recon mission. We are there for intel and to get whatever else we can. I'll give you further instructions later before we depart."

"Got it Dad. How long will this mission last?"

"About three months. I'll tell Ryan when we get back."

"Can Ryan come this time? Please dad? I missed him too much last time."

"We gotta ask him. It would be his decision." Zaya smiles and walks off.

We both had a few things we needed to do after our meeting with the council. We completed those tasks and picked up Ryan for dinner. We went to a fancy restaurant.

"Hey little brother." Zaya smiles. "You wanna come on a recon mission with us?" Ryan fills his mouth with food.

"Sure. I have been training. I wanna test my limits. So, if we run into any enemy, let me handle them."

"Deal!" Zaya held her cup up and suggested that we make a toast. We held up our cups. She quietly shouted, "To the family that never stops going!"

We all downed our drinks as the server asked us to lower our noise levels. The burning effect hit all of our chests at the same time. 5 started laughing.

"Y'all first drinks were with your old man."

Zaya replied laughing stronger,

"Not exactly dad. We had our first drinks with the bbq. Remember?"

5 responded, "Ohhhhh yeahhhhh."

All of us laughed almost uncontrollably together for several minutes. The server overheard this and laughed with us. What a sight this was for us all.

(…Meanwhile Freya and Zero)

In the Invitca territory, Freya and Zero had the same dream. They both woke up in cold sweats. What could this mean? How did it happen? Freya asked herself, "What is going on?" She grabbed her body as if it was to make sure she was still alive.

"What happened?" She asked herself over and over.

Zero, before he woke up in his cold sweat, was trapped in the nightmare. He couldn't wake up because he thought his dream was reality. He had lived out the pain of losing everyone once so it gripped him and trapped him. When he finally woke up it was still time before the morning run. He was drenched in tears and cold sweat. He realized it was just a dream, but also a warning.

"I must talk to mom." He thought as the chief yelled,

"GET UP MAGGOTS! TIME TO RUN!!"

(…Meanwhile back home.)

Ryan and Zaya got ready and packed their bags.

"You should go tell Lily that you will be back in three months."

"I will." Ryan replied.

"She looks like she might be pregnant. What did y'all do?" Dad asked.

"Nothing." Ryan nervously replied.

Ryan went and spoke to Lily.

"I miss you already Ryan. Please be safe and come back to me. I love you so much."

"Lily, I miss you already too. I'll be safe. I didn't train all this time for nothing. We'll be back in three months."

"Well Ryan, I'll have your return date marked on my calendar."

"I love you Lily." We started kissing and afterwards I went home to prepare for my first recon mission.

After Ryan finished packing, he shared.

"Hey, I had another dream where we all died. I am worried about it, but..."

"...Let's head out you guys." 5 says interrupting Ryan as he grabbed his gear.

"Now, what were you saying son?" Dad asked.

"I'll tell you later dad. Okay? Let's head out."

Ryan suggested as he grabbed his gear. Zaya also grabbed her gear. They all stood still for a moment in silence holding their gear. Everyone had the same facial expression: focused concern. 5 opened the door exiting their home. Ryan and Zaya followed. After they passed their father, 5 locked the door.

We headed out on our recon mission.

To be continued in...

THE OBLITERATION

QUENTIN A. BOSTON

UNFAZED PUBLISHING
YOUR MIND IS OUR BUSINESS

BECOME AN AUTHOR WITH US.

SET UP A FREE WRITING CONSULTATION TODAY.

www.UnFazedPublishing.com

www.ingramcontent.com/pod-product-compliance
Lightning Source LLC
Chambersburg PA
CBHW071345170626
46811CB00003B/992

* 9 7 8 1 9 5 9 2 7 5 2 7 5 *